# YASMIN

## The Friend

written by
### SAADIA FARUQI

To Mariam for inspiring me, and Mubashir
for helping me find the right words – S.F.

To my sister, Eman, and her amazing girls,
Jana and Kenzi – H.A.

Raintree is an imprint of Capstone Global Library Limited, a company
incorporated in England and Wales having its registered office at
264 Banbury Road, Oxford, OX2 7DY – Registered company number:
6695582

www.raintree.co.uk
myorders@raintree.co.uk

Text © Capstone Global Library Limited 2021
The moral rights of the proprietor have been asserted.

Edited by Kristen Mohn
Designed by Lori Bye and Kay Fraser
Original illustrations © Capstone Global Library Limited 2021
Picture research by Jo Miller
Production by Tori Abraham
Originated by Capstone Global Library Ltd

978 1 4747 9364 3

**British Library Cataloguing in Publication Data**
A full catalogue record for this book is available from the British
Library.

**Acknowledgements**
Design Elements: Shutterstock: Art and Fashion, rangsan paidaen.

Printed and bound in India

# TABLE OF CONTENTS

Chapter 1
GUESTS......................................................5

Chapter 2
A FIGHT BETWEEN FRIENDS.................10

Chapter 3
A NEW GAME ........................................16

# CHAPTER 1

# Guests

Yasmin was excited. Ali and Emma were coming over to play.

"I want to have a perfect day," she told Baba. "I will plan lots of fun things to do and yummy snacks to eat."

"Sounds great," Baba agreed. "But don't forget to ask your friends what they would like to do. Friends are a blessing. We should make them happy."

Yasmin brought her box of dressing-up clothes into the living room. "We're going to have so much fun!" she sang.

Ali arrived first. He had a bag

of small balls with him. "I'm

learning to juggle," he said.

"You didn't have to bring

your toys," Yasmin said to Ali. "I

have lots of things to play with."

Then Emma arrived. She held up a new skipping rope. "My uncle gave this to me for my birthday," she said. "Isn't it great?"

## CHAPTER 2

# A fight
# between friends

Yasmin opened her box of dressing-up clothes. She held up a unicorn suit.

"Let's dress up," she said. "Nani made these costumes for me. What do you want to wear?"

Ali headed for the back
garden. "Nah! I want to juggle.
I'm going to be a famous juggler
when I grow up."

Yasmin frowned. She and
Emma followed Ali outside.

They watched as Ali threw the balls in the air. One by one they landed on the ground.

One hit him on the nose.

"Ha!" Emma laughed. "You need lots of practice."

She started to skip with her rope. "Yasmin, count how many times I can jump."

Yasmin shook her head.

"But I want to play dressing up,"

she complained.

She didn't

think Ali and

Emma were

being very

good friends.

Ali crossed his arms over
his chest. "I don't want to skip
or play dressing up. I'd rather
juggle."

Yasmin watched as her
friends played by themselves.

Ali juggled by the bushes.

Emma skipped. "One, two,
three, four!"

Yasmin groaned. Why didn't
anyone want to play dressing up
with her?

## CHAPTER 3

# A new game

Baba helped Yasmin make a tray of snacks. There were cookies and gajar to eat. There was mango lassi to drink.

"I'm sure they'll fight over what to eat too," Yasmin grumbled.

Baba patted Yasmin's shoulder. "Remember to think about what your friends want. Not just what you want, jaan."

Yasmin looked out of the window at Emma and Ali.

*How can I get my friends to play together?* Yasmin wondered.

Then she saw two squirrels jump over one another, carrying acorns. Yasmin's eyes grew wide.

"I have an idea!" she shouted.

"What's your idea?" Baba
asked.

"You'll see!" Yasmin said and
ran outside.

"Let's play Juggle Jump!"

Yasmin said to Emma and Ali.

Emma stopped jumping.

"How do you play that?"

"We skip with the rope
while juggling balls. We count
how many times we can jump
without dropping the balls,"
Yasmin explained.

"Sounds fun," Ali said.
"Bonus points if you wear
a costume!"

They took turns twirling the
rope and juggling and jumping.
It was so much fun!

Soon they fell down on the grass, laughing.

Baba came outside with the tray.

"Snacks!" the kids cheered. "Thank you!"

"Juggle Jump was a great idea, Yasmin," Ali said while they ate.

"Yes!" Emma agreed. "It's more fun when friends play together!"

# Think about it, talk about it

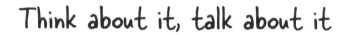

* What games do you like to play with your friends? What activities do you like to do when you're playing by yourself? What is different about playing with a friend?

* Yasmin's dad says that friends are a blessing. What do you think he means by this?

* What are some ways you can be a good host when you have friends to visit? How do you like to be treated when you are at a friend's house?

# Learn Urdu with Yasmin!

Yasmin's family speaks both English and Urdu. Urdu is a language from Pakistan. Maybe you already know some Urdu words!

**baba**  father

**gajar**  carrots

**hijab**  scarf covering the hair

**jaan**  life; a sweet nickname for a loved one

**lassi**  yogurt drink

**mama**  mother

**nana**  grandfather on mother's side

**nani**  grandmother on mother's side

**salaam**  hello

**shukriya**  thank you

# Pakistani fun facts

Yasmin and her family are proud of their Pakistani culture. Yasmin loves to share facts about Pakistan!

### Location

Pakistan is on the continent of Asia, with India on one side and Afghanistan on the other.

### Population

Pakistan's population is more than 200,000,000 people. It is the world's sixth-most-populated country.

### Fun and adventure

In Pakistan, football is a popular sport among boys and girls.

The first Pakistani to travel to the North and South Poles is a young woman called Namira Salim.

# Make a plastic bag skipping rope

## SUPPLIES:

- 10–12 used plastic bags of different colours
- scissors
- strong tape

## STEPS:

1. Cut the bags open and lay them flat.

2. Cut the handles off so that each bag is a large, rectangular piece.

3. Cut each rectangle into several strips of plastic.

4. Tie the strips together end-to-end to make a long plastic rope. Make it slightly longer than you'd like your skipping rope to be.

5. Repeat this until you have nine long, colourful ropes.

6. Tape the ends of three of the ropes together. Then plait the ropes. Tape the other ends together when done. Repeat this process with the other ropes to make three plaits in total.

7. Now plait the three ropes together into one strong rope.

8. Wrap the ends in strong tape to make handles for the skipping rope.

Saadia Faruqi is a Pakistani American writer, interfaith activist and cultural sensitivity trainer previously profiled in *O Magazine*. She is editor-in-chief of *Blue Minaret*, a magazine for Muslim art, poetry and prose. Saadia is also author of the adult short story collection, *Brick Walls: Tales of Hope & Courage from Pakistan*. Her essays have been published in *Huffington Post*, *Upworthy* and *NBC Asian America*. She lives in Texas, USA, with her husband and children.

Hatem Aly is an Egyptian-born illustrator whose work has been featured in multiple publications worldwide. He currently lives in beautiful New Brunswick, Canada, with his wife, son and more pets than people. When he is not dipping cookies in a cup of tea or staring at blank pieces of paper, he is usually drawing books. One of the books he illustrated is *The Inquisitor's Tale* by Adam Gidwitz, which won a Newbery Honor and other awards, despite Hatem's drawings of a farting dragon, a two-headed cat and stinky cheese.

# Join Yasmin on all her adventures!

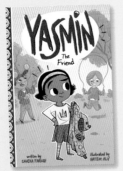

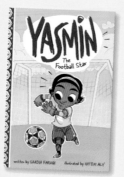

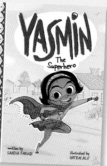

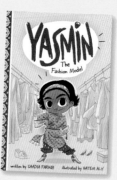
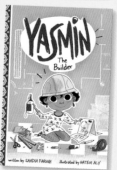
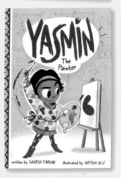